D0405743

Dear Parent:

Psst . . . you're looking at the Super Secret Weapon of Reading. It's called comics.

STEP INTO READING® COMIC READERS are a perfect step in learning to read. They provide visual cues to the meaning of words and helpfully break out short pieces of dialogue into speech balloons.

Here are some terms commonly associated with comics:
PANEL: A section of a comic with a box drawn around it.
CAPTION: Narration that helps set the scene.
SPEECH BALLOON: A bubble containing dialogue.
GUTTER: The space between panels.

Tips for reading comics with your child:

- **Have your child read the speech balloons while you read the captions.**
- **Ask your child: What is a character feeling? How can you tell?**
- **Have your child draw a comic showing what happens after the book is finished.**

STEP INTO READING® COMIC READERS are designed to engage and to provide an empowering reading experience. They are also fun. The best-kept secret of comics is that they create lifelong readers. ***And that will make you the real hero of the story!***

Jennifer L. Holm and Matthew Holm
Co-creators of the Babymouse and Squish series

Special thanks to Diane Reichenberger, Cindy Ledermann, Jocelyn Morgan, Tanya Mann, Emily Kelly, Sharon Woloszyk, Michelle Cogan, Allison Monterosso, David Wiebe, and ARC Productions.

www.barbie.com
Published in the United States by Random House Children's Books, a division of Random House, Inc., 1745 Broadway, New York, NY 10019, and in Canada by Random House of Canada Limited, Toronto.

Visit us on the Web!
StepIntoReading.com
randomhouse.com/kids

Educators and librarians, for a variety of teaching tools, visit us at RHTeachersLibrarians.com

ISBN 978-0-385-37121-6 (trade) — ISBN 978-0-375-97187-7 (lib. bdg.)

Printed in the United States of America 10 9 8 7 6 5 4 3 2 1

STEP INTO READING® STEP 3

Adapted by Kristen L. Depken

Based on the screenplay by Robin Stein

Random House New York

The Dreamhouse is so amazing!

At the Dreamhouse, Nikki and Teresa are helping Barbie pick out an outfit.

Chic or so last-week?

Both.

How is it chic *and* so last-week?

Last week was a really good week for me.

I love this outfit! I want to look perfect for my date with Ken.

It's our forty-third anniversary!

Huh?
What?

It's the forty-third anniversary of the first time we held hands!

You can't find a greeting card for that!

Barbie can't wait for her date!
Her outfit is almost perfect.

My little rhinestone-studded butterfly barrette.

It's right here in my closet.

Barbie's closet . . .

is . . .

AMAZING!

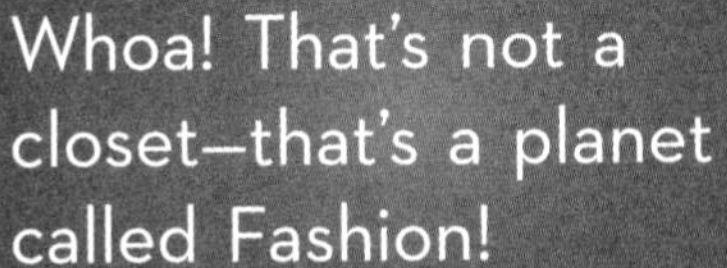
Whoa! That's not a closet—that's a planet called Fashion!

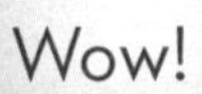
Wow!

Whoa!
Oh, it's just a few odds and ends.

Meanwhile . . .

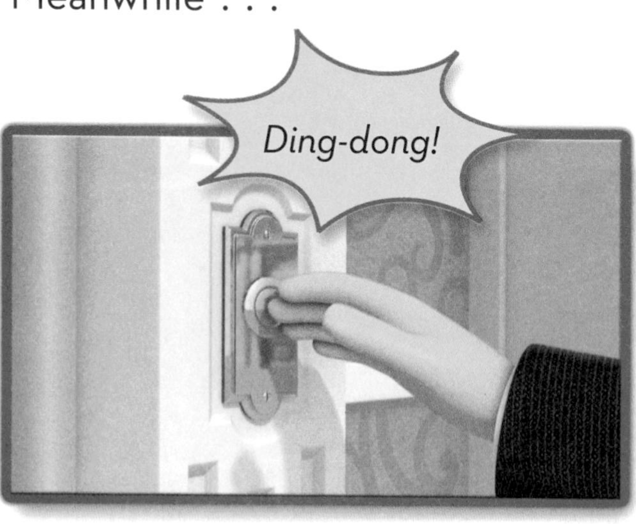

Minty fresh!

I'm so excited!

Barbie gives Teresa and Nikki a tour of her closet.

You went to the moon?

You haven't?

Hmm . . .

That skirt rocks!
Can I borrow it?

Of course!

Knock yourselves out!

Oooh, a belt to go with my new jeans . . .
. . . and every pair of pants I've ever owned!

Yay!
Yay!

Is Barbie not the coolest friend ever?
She's fun, generous . . .
. . . and exactly my size!

How did my bag get so heavy?
This way to the makeup room.

Whoa, Barbie. I mean this in the best possible way—you've got a big head!

They get right to work. . . .

Hours later . . .

Back in the closet . . .

Barbie, how much farther?

Yeah, we're exhausted!

A day or two's walk,
tops! I promise!

We're
famished!

And starving.

I may have a mint in my pocket.

Ohhhhhhhh! Here's my barrette! Isn't that funny?

You had it the whole time?

We came all this way for nothing?

And I found this cute necklace that will really put my outfit over the top.

Yes, but . . .
I want out of here!

Yeah! I canceled a yoga lesson for this.
Or was it a yogurt lesson?

What's this?
Who cares? Pull it!

Nooo!

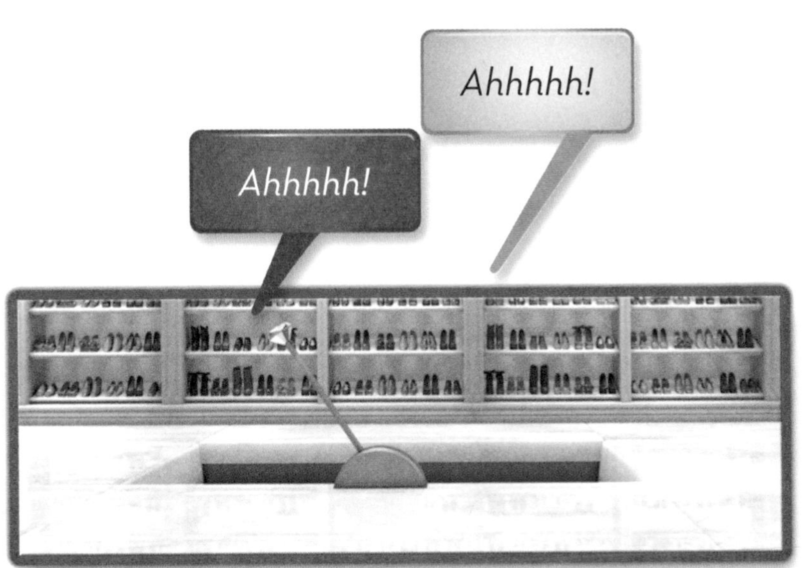

Ahhhhh!
Ahhhhh!

They slide
down a long dark chute . . .

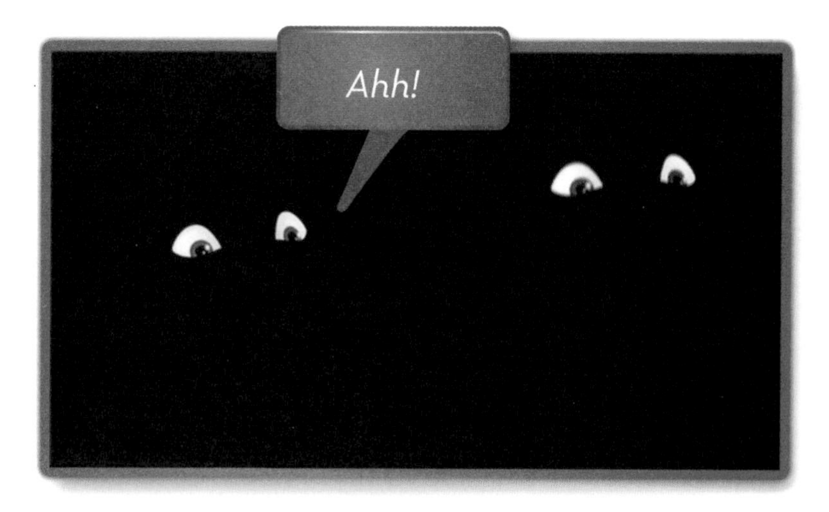

and land on Barbie's front steps!

Ken?

Is Barbie ready
for our date yet?

Ta-da! I sure am!

Happy anniversary,
Barbie!
Ohh, Ken!

Yum!
Yum!

Thanks for all your help, girls! You're the best friends ever!

Thanks!
I love the stubble!